RITA DAS
•
AVNI DAS

SCHOLASTIC
New York Toronto London Auckland
Sydney New Delhi Hong Kong

Rita Das is a passionate teacher by profession and has a big heart for the tiny tots. She enjoys making creative artefacts for children. She wears her imagination cap all the time and loves taking on art and craft projects using anything and everything.

Avni Das is a techie by profession, but artistic by nature. She enjoys creating decorations with easy-to-do, low cost, easily available materials.

Published by Scholastic India Pvt. Ltd.
A subsidiary of Scholastic Inc., New York, 10012 (USA).
Publishers since 1920, with international operations in Canada, Australia, New Zealand, the United Kingdom, India, and Hong Kong.

For information regarding permission, write to:
Scholastic India Pvt. Ltd.
A-27, Ground Floor, Bharti Sigma Centre
Infocity-1, Sector 34, Gurgaon 122001 (India)

First edition: May 2014

ISBN-13: 978-93-5103-275-5

Printed at Shivam Offset Press, New Delhi.

Contents

FOR 'YOU' – THE YOUNG CREATIVE DESIGNER!

This is a craft book specially written for you to enjoy and bring out your creativity. It is packed with many interesting things for you to make, with easily available things.

Every craft item in this book has three parts—supplies needed, steps to make the craft project and the patterns or templates, as required. At several places specific measurements are omitted specifically, leaving the total creative process to the young designers!

We recommend you read all steps carefully before getting started. Do collect all the things you'll require before you begin. An adult's help may come in handy while undertaking difficult tasks like tracing the pattern, enlarging the templates, cutting or doing anything else. Take your time with the project. Your own creativity will add a personal touch to each craft project you make. Think of this book as a chocolate layered-cake, where one slice is never enough!

Happy Craft Time!!

TOP CRAFT

1 Table Decorations

2 Make Your Own Toys

3 Gifting Is Fun

4 Fun With Weather

5 Home Decorations

Table Decorations

Iris Paper Flowers

These delightful flowers are quite easy to make. Just trace the pattern or resize it to suit your requirement. Paint, add a few stems and leaves and voila, your cool bunch of delicate irises is ready.

You will need

- Scissors
- Plain paper (not too thick)
- Tracing paper
- Poster paint (any pastel shade)
- Paint brushes
- A pencil
- Thin sticks painted green (optional)

Get started

1. Trace the flower pattern on plain paper (on page 48) and cut it out.

2. Paint or colour both sides, in a colour of your choice.

3. Curl petals A, C and E upwards using a pencil.

4. Curl remaining three petals (B, D, F) downward.

5. Paint a thin stick green and push it through the flower.

Alternative: Use coloured poster paper instead of painting the petals.

Christmas Tree

Create your own spirally Christmas tree and get into the festive spirit.

Get started

You will need:

- Green cartridge sheet
- Green straws
- One wooden skewer
- Thick thermacol (approx. 2"x2")
- Scissors
- Gold / Silver paper (for the star)
- Red craft clay

1. Cut nine to 10 circular discs of graduating size from the green cartridge sheet.

2. Use a pair of pinking shears, or just snip around the outside edge of the discs, to create a zigzag pattern.

3. Make nine round balls of red clay.

4. Start by pushing one small round ball of clay, followed by the biggest disc, through the skewer. Repeat the process, alternating between the balls of clay and paper discs, graduating from the biggest to the smallest circle.

5. Now push the tree through the spool base.

6. Cut two stars and place it on the top of the tree. Paste the two stars with the skewer threading through the centre.

Papier Mâché Spider

Jazz up your study table top with this cute handmade spider, or just use it as a paper weight.

You will need

- Newspaper (six to eight, full-size, non-glossy sheets)
- Water
- Small tub or bucket
- Craft glue
- Bright fabric paint
- Brush
- Googly eyes
- 4 'U' hair pins (for tentacles)

Get started

1. Tear the sheets of newspaper into small pieces.
2. Pour enough water, in a tub or a bucket, to soak the newspaper for four to five days.
3. Keep turning and churning the paper every day.
4. On the fifth day, knead the paper into pulp.
5. Make a ball (size of a cricket ball) out of the pulp. Squeeze out the excess water.
6. Add about 100 grams of craft glue to the pulp. Mix and keep it aside.
7. Take four 'U' hair pins (used for making hair buns) and break them into eight equal parts.
8. Bend the pins in the centre to give them a little curve.
9. Push the pins into the papier mâché ball while still wet.
10. Allow it to dry.
11. Paint the spider and paste the googly eyes.

Pet Porcupine

Ever thought of having your own fun pet? Here's how to make a neat and easy porcupine with toothpicks and paper. Watch your prickly pet come alive!

You will need

- ⊃ Light brown A4 size cartridge sheet
- ⊃ Dark brown and black poster paint
- ⊃ Brush
- ⊃ Toothpicks
- ⊃ Craft glue

Get started

1. Take half a box of toothpicks and paint them black. Keep them aside to dry.

2. On the light brown A4 size sheet draw the outline of a porcupine.

3. Paint the porcupine with dark brown poster paint.

4. Paste the black toothpicks as shown to depict the spines of the porcupine and your pet porcupine is ready.

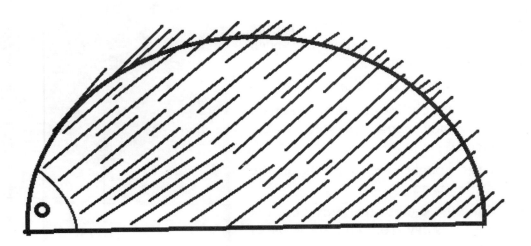

Turtle Paper Weight

Here is a cute little turtle paper weight to keep papers from flying around. A great gift for your mom or dad!

You will need

- 2 empty half walnut shells
- Plaster of Paris
- Green handmade paper
- Scissors
- Craft glue
- 2 small googly eyes or black beads

Get started

1. Mix one tablespoon of water to three tablespoons of Plaster of Paris to prepare a thick mixture.

2. Fill both the walnut shells with the Plaster of Paris which has been mixed with water.

3. Place it in the sun to dry.

4. Draw the outline of a turtle on green handmade paper, as seen in the picture.

5. Paste googly eyes or beads on the turtle's head.

6. Glue the shell to the body once the plaster is dry. Your cute turtle paper weight is ready!

Table Decorations

Stained Glass Photo Frame

Frame a special photograph in this lovely frame! It becomes a perfect handmade gift too!

You will need

- Cardboard
- Ruler
- Scissors
- Foil
- Craft glue
- Permanent marker
- OHP transparency sheet
- Stained glass outliner
- Stained glass paints
- Wide Cello tape (1.5 cm thickness)

Get started

1. Measure and cut out a cardboard frame for the photograph you would like to frame. Make sure it is a few centimeters larger than the photo.

2. Cut the foil. It should be bigger than the cardboard frame. Gently crush it for a wrinkly feel.

3. Spread craft glue on the cardboard frame and stick the foil over it. Tuck the edges in well, smoothening the foil carefully.

4. Place the photograph in the centre of the frame and cover the back with foil-covered cardboard.

5. Take an OHP sheet (easily available at the stationery shop) and cut it precisely to fit the foil-covered frame.

6. Draw flowers and leaves (or whatever you wish to), big enough to be outlined and painted, with the help of a thin permanent marker. Outline the drawing with the stained glass outliner. (TIP: you can use a glitter tube instead of the glass outliner)

7. Once the outline has dried completely, paint the flowers and leaves, and allow it to dry.

8. With a wide cello tape, neatly attach the OHP sheet to the foil covered frame.

Leather Effect Flower Vase

Make best out of waste and create your own flower vase in a jiffy. Fill it up with flowers and you will have spring on your table everyday.

You will need

- 1 litre empty bottle (liquid detergent or shampoo bottle)
- Wide white masking tape (also called paper tape)
- Dark brown oil pastel crayon

Get started

1. Take an empty bottle and cut out the top to have a wide mouth to put some flowers in.
2. Stick one inch long strips of masking tape all over the bottle. Make sure the strips overlap each other and cover every inch of the bottle.
3. Now rub a dark brown oil pastel crayon over the masking tape covered bottle.
4. Your vase has a subtle leathery effect. Put in some bright flowers and you are ready to go.

Juice Carton Santa

'Ho, ho, ho!' This easy-to-make, cool Santa will put you in the festive spirit.

You will need

- One litre empty juice carton
- Coloured paper (pink, red, black and white) or plain paper with red and pink paints and brush
- Craft glue
- 15-20 white cotton balls
- Artificial or real poinsettias

Get started

1. Wash an empty juice carton and cut off the top.

2. Cover the carton with pink paper or paint it pink.

3. Around the top of the carton, paste a red strip of paper or paint it red.

4. Glue the cotton balls to the bottom half of the carton.

5. Cut a moustache and eyebrows from white paper and paste them on the top.

6. Now cut out two black circles for eyes, a red circle for the nose, two pink cheeks and a red mouth. Paste them on the carton (as shown in the illustration).

7. Put plastic or real poinsettias into the carton. For real flowers, add a little water to the carton.

PoP Bug Magnets

Make some bright bug magnets and show them off on your fridge, cupboard or mirror.

You will need

- ⊃ 1 tablespoon of plaster of paris (PoP)
- ⊃ Water
- ⊃ Matchsticks or toothpicks
- ⊃ 2 googly eyes
- ⊃ Magnet
- ⊃ Neon fabric paint (orange and black)
- ⊃ Paint brush
- ⊃ 1 plastic tablespoon

Get started

1. In a small bowl, mix the Plaster of Paris and enough water to make a thick mixture.

2. Quickly pour the batter in a plastic tablespoon. Tap it gently to spread the PoP evenly and level the spoon.

3. When the PoP is still wet, break the toothpicks into two and push four pieces into the PoP to make the bug's legs.

4. Let it dry for an hour in the sun.

5. Invert the spoon and tap it gently to get the bug out.

6. Let it dry completely before you paint the bug with the neon paints.

7. Stick two small googly eyes.

8. Glue the magnet on the reverse side.

9. Your magnet bug is ready.

Alternative: If you are unable to find a magnet of the size of the bug, you can use double-sided tape and stick it on any surface.

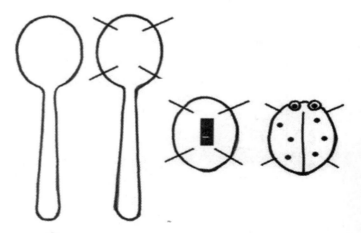

TOP CRAFT

1 Table Decorations

2 Make Your Own Toys

Make Your Own Toys

3 Gifting Is Fun

4 Fun With Weather

5 Home Decorations

Caterpillar Arm Puppet

Puppets are great fun! They don't cost much and are easy to make. Here's how to make a caterpillar arm puppet. Make your own puppet theatre and enjoy.

You will need

- Any shade of green, yellow or orange handmade paper
- White and black paper for the eyes
- Craft glue
- Scissors

Get started

1. Using the template on page 49 (scale to make it big enough to cover your palm to mid arm), cut out two caterpillar shapes from the coloured handmade paper.

2. Stick only the edges of both the caterpillar shapes together, leaving one side open to put your arm inside.

3. Paste the eyes.

4. Cut four to five uneven dots of various sizes and paste them on the paper.

5. Wear your caterpillar puppet on your arm and enjoy reciting a poem or make up your own story!

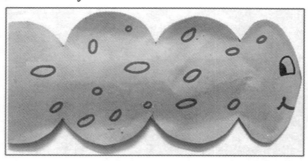

Beads in the Cup

Improve your eye and hand coordination and concentration with this easy to make traditional game.

You will need

- A thermocol glass
- Crayons or paints to decorate the glass
- One bead
- Thread (10" to 12" approximately)

Get started

1. In a thermocol glass, punch a hole on the side.

2. Draw and decorate the glass with crayons or paints.

3. Pass the thread through the hole and tie it.

4. Tie a bead to the other end of the thread.

5. Now move the glass to and fro and try to put the bead into the glass.

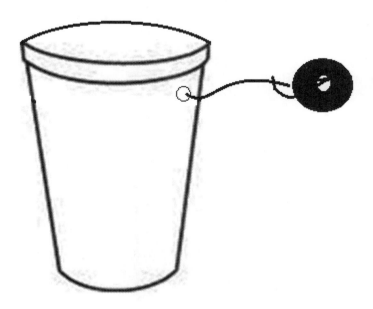

Dancing Snake

Be a snake charmer and watch this paper snake dance to your tune.

You will need

- ➲ A wooden or a plastic spool
- ➲ One sharpened pencil
- ➲ Plain white card paper
- ➲ Colours to paint the snake
- ➲ Scissors

Get started

1. Cut a spiral snake, long enough to cover the pencil (template on page 50).

2. Place a sharpened pencil in the hole of the spool (shown in the picture).

3. Now put the tip of the cut spiral snake on the pencil point.

4. Watch the snake dance when you place the spool on the floor, under the ceiling fan.

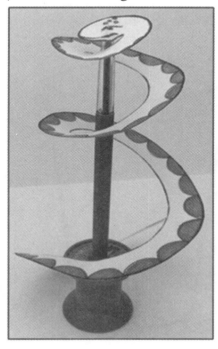

Paper Plate Magnet

This is a fun motor skill development game that is perfect for all ages.

You will need

- ⊃ Sturdy white paper plate
- ⊃ Crayons/ paints
- ⊃ Small, shiny star stickers
- ⊃ Two magnets (one small, the other bigger with a hole at the centre)
- ⊃ Yarn (long enough to be able to move over the plate)

Get started

1. Paint the white paper plate a dark midnight blue, for the night sky.

2. Paste the small silver stars.

3. Punch a hole on the side of the plate.

4. Take a yarn and tie a knot on one end. Tie the magnet with a hole to the other end.

5. Take the smaller magnet and place it on the plate.

6. Using the bigger magnet (tied to the yarn), try to move the smaller magnet on the plate, making sure that you don't touch the stars.

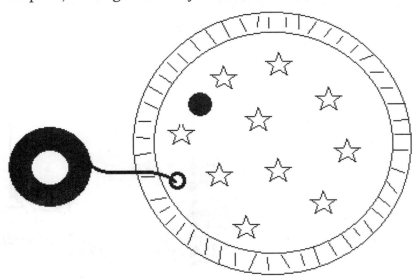

Rhythmic Noise Maker

Let's make a musical instrument and some music with pebbles, beans and maybe even macaroni!

You will need

- ⊃ 2 small paper tea cups (same size)
- ⊃ A wooden tongue depressor (used by doctors to check your tongue, available at medical stores)
- ⊃ Wide paper tape
- ⊃ A handful of small pebbles, beans or macaroni
- ⊃ Crayons or paints
- ⊃ Self-sticking beads

Get started

1. Paint the cup and decorate it with beads on the outside.

2. Put the pebbles, beans or macaroni in one cup.

3. Place the open ends of the cups together and tape them together with paper tape, leaving about an inch un-taped.

4. The tongue depressor makes a good handle. Insert it in the un-taped space between the cups. (If you can't find a tongue depressor, just stick two-three ice cream sticks together).

5. Now, tape it once again, such that the contents of the cup don't fall out.

6. To play, shake the maracas in the air, to the beat of lively music. Make two rhythmic noise makers and have lots of fun.

TAPE

Flying Black Bat

This flying bat can be hung from the window or you could run with it and watch it bounce behind you.

You will need

- ⊃ A pencil
- ⊃ String
- ⊃ Tracing paper
- ⊃ Black thick craft sheet (A4 size)
- ⊃ A thin rubber band about 2" to 3" long

Get started

1. Trace the outline of the bat on a tracing paper. (Template on page 52).

2. Fold the black paper in half and keep the tracing paper on top of the black paper. Ensure that the lower part of the bat's body is on the fold line.

3. Trace the outline of the bat onto the black paper. Make sure you press hard enough for the impressions to show on the black paper.

4. Cut out the bat, with the lower body on the folded side. Poke a small hole through the wings, on the top.

5. Cut the rubber band and thread it through the holes in the wings. Tie a knot at each end of the rubber band and open the bat.

6. Pull it to make the bat fly and bounce.

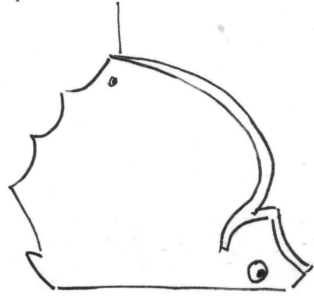

...ng Monkey

...ike to see monkeys jump from one tree to another. Let's make a
...y to play with..

You will need

- ⊃ One unsharpened pencil
- ⊃ Monkey pattern
- ⊃ Craft glue
- ⊃ Brown crayon
- ⊃ Scissors

Get started

1. Cut the monkey pattern (on page 53).

2. Paste the parts appropriately.

3. Colour the monkey.

4. Roll the hands on the pencil.

5. Twirl the pencil and see the monkey tumble again and again.

Make Your Own Toys

Parrot in a Cage

Here's a simple toy that uses optical illusion to trick the eye.

You will need

- Cardboard 6 x 6 inches
- Parrot template
- Crayons
- Craft glue
- Scissors
- Strong yarn (36 inches)

Get Started

1. Draw and colour the picture of the parrot (template on page 54) but not the cage.

2. Cut both the circles.

3. Paste one circle on the cardboard and cut it out once it dries.

4. Paste the other circle on the other side.

5. With a pointed object, make four holes on the disc (as marked).

6. Thread a 18" yarn through the disc and tie it as shown in the picture.

7. Hold the thread from the end, twirl it and release it.

8. It will look like a bird in a cage.

Flying Fish

Can you make fish swim in the air? Do this activity to find out.

You will need

- Thin postcard type paper (any colour)
- A white sheet (A4 size)
- Pencil
- Scissors
- Dowel stick or a thin twig
- Thick thread or yarn

Get Started

1. Draw a fish on any coloured paper (template on page 55).
2. Cut the fish into five parts.
3. Glue three strips of A4 white paper or colour it blue and then paste it as shown, leaving a little space.
4. String the parts to hang from the dowel stick as shown.

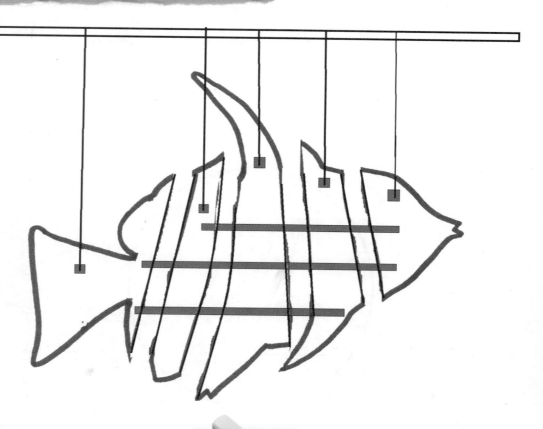

Make Your Own Toys

TOP CRAFT

1 Table Decorations

2 Make Your Own Toys

3 Gifting Is Fun

Gifting Is Fun

4 Fun With Weather

5 Home Decorations

Cool Card

Emails and text messages may be the preferred choice for wishing friends and family on special occasions these days, but there is still nothing more charming than receiving a greeting card.

You will need

⊃ Cello tape
⊃ OHP transparency sheet or clear thick plastic sheet
⊃ Glitter tubes
⊃ Permanent marker (black)
⊃ Craft paper (thick paper)

Get started

1. With the help of a permanent marker, draw the outline of any object on the OHP sheet (use stencils if necessary). Make sure the outline is neat.

2. Fill in glitter paints and let it dry completely.

3. Choose any bright coloured paper or card as the background of your OHP sheet painting. Use cello tape to neatly stick the OHP painting on the card.

4. Your cool card is ready.

Friendship Bands

Friends are for eternity. Make these easy-to-make bands for your BFFs and make them feel special.

You will need

- Coloured foam sheets (easily available) or thick handmade paper
- Craft glue
- Scissors
- Single hole paper punch
- 2 lengths of yarn

Get started

1. Cut out a five to six inch long strip of foam and adjust its size according to that of your wrist.

2. Cut out small patterns from the different coloured foam sheets and stick these on the long strip of foam.

3. Punch two holes on each side.

4. Pass the yarn through the holes (as shown) to tie around the wrist.

Alternatives: Use plain foam or handmade paper for the band and stick glitter foam on it for decoration.

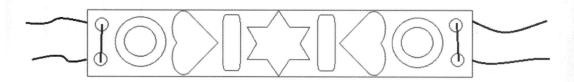

Bookmarks for Bookworms

Customise bookmarks for your friends and family. Draw their favourite objects, initials or just about anything.

You will need

⊃ Stiff card paper
⊃ Scissors
⊃ Pencil
⊃ Ruler

Get started

1. Use a pencil to outline the boat or any other shape for the top of the bookmark. Cut out the bookmark. cut it out.

2. Use a sketch pen to colour in the design and draw a neat border with a sketch pen.

Tip: You could even cut along the dotted lines to insert the bookmark onto the page.

Happy Reading!!

Gifting Is Fun

Eggshell Tulips

A bunch of flowers is a treat for the eyes. Make a whole bouquet, without plucking out a single flower from the garden.

You will need

- Empty egg shells
- Thin permanent marker
- Drinking straw (green)
- Green thick chart paper (A4 size)
- Craft glue
- Red fabric paint
- Paint brush
- Small ball of clay
- Scissors

Get started

1. Gently crack the egg shell from the bottom. Be careful not to break the egg (the crack should be just enough to push a straw in).

2. Drain out the egg and wash the egg shell with water. Do not use soap. Let it dry.

3. Push the straw through the hole into the egg.

4. Hold the egg by the straw and paint it red. Let it dry.

5. Once dry, draw petals with a permanent marker.

6. Push the straw into a chunk of clay so that it makes a flower stand.

7. Cut leaves from a chart paper and glue or staple them to the straw.

8. Now make a bouquet of flowers.

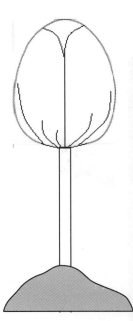

Floating Ducks in a Pond

Make a duck family (which is called a brace of ducks) and watch them float in a pool of water.

You will need

- One large thermocol dinner plate or a pie dish
- White card paper
- Scissors
- Crayons/ paints
- Craft glue
- Water for the ducks to float in

Get started

1. Draw the ducks on white card paper (template on page 51).
2. Fold along the dotted lines so that there is a base for the duck to float on.
3. Colour the ducks on both sides.
4. Cut out the duck shapes except for the heads as these will be pasted together.
5. Paster the two heads craft glue paste the two head togerther.
6. Now put some water in the plate and see if your ducks float.

Gift one to your friend.

Fun With Weather

Paper Helicopter

Bored on a windy day? Have some fun with this amazing paper helicopter!

You will need

- ⊃ White paper (thin enough for tracing)
- ⊃ Thin craft paper (any colour)
- ⊃ Ruler
- ⊃ Paper Clips
- ⊃ Pencil

Get started

1. Trace the pattern on white paper (pattern on page 57). Transfer to cartridge paper.

2. Cut the pattern.

3. Fold one wing forward and the other back.

4. Fold the tabs back, so that they overlap. Slip clips over the tabs.

5. Now raise your arms and release your helicopter in the air. Watch it twirl to the ground.

Tip: Fly it outdoors on a windy day for some extra action.

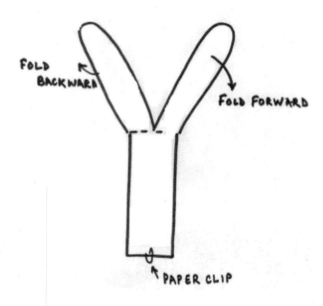

FOLD BACKWARD

FOLD FORWARD

PAPER CLIP

Thermocol Twig Raft

Create a raft that floats, using twigs gathered from your garden.

You will need

- Thin thermocol piece (6 x 4 inches)
- Dry twigs (enough to cover the thermocol)
- Thick paper to make a flag of any colour you desire.

Get started

1. Stick the twigs on the thermocol, close enough to cover it completely.

2. Take one twig (approximately 10 inches) and paste a triangular paper on the top, for the sail.

3. Push it in the centre between the twigs and into the thermocol (as shown). Voila! Your raft is ready to float.

Place the raft in a water-filled tub and manoeuvre it with a straw.

Sunny Day Hat

Make yourself a matching bonnet and save yourself from the sun on a hot sunny day.

You will need

- A sturdy, full-size thermocol or paper plate
- Scissors
- Satin ribbon (any colour)
- Paper flowers and leaves

Get started

1. To begin, cut slits (1 inch long) at opposite end of the plate's rim.
2. Cut a ribbon about 36 inches in length, to tie under your chin.
3. Push each side of the ribbon through a slit. (The ribbon should stretch across the underside of the plate.)
4. Tape, staple or glue the ribbon on the hat.
5. Decorate the hat with flowers and leaves.

Carrot Sun Catcher

A pretty looking sun catcher that helps you catch the rays of sunlight as they filter into your room.

You will need

- ⊃ Butter/Wax paper
- ⊃ Orange flourescent poster paint
- ⊃ Green flourescent poster paint
- ⊃ Craft glue
- ⊃ Green and orange yarn (10 inches each)

Get started

1. Take a piece of butter or wax paper (approximately 8 x 6 inches) and trace the pattern given on page 56).

2. Paste the orange yarn such that it outlines the carrot.

3. Paste the green yarn on the outlines of the leaves.

4. Mix the orange flourescent poster paint with craft glue to get the desired shade.

5. Paint the carrot with a thin layer of the paint mix.

6. Now, mix the green flourescent poster paint with craft glue and fill the leaves with a thin layer.

7. When the glue is completely dry, peel it off from the wax paper.

8. Place the leaves on the carrot and hang the carrot sun catcher with a string on a sunlit window and watch it shine.

Make as many carrots or any other vegetable/fruit that you like.

Jingle Bells

Why wait for Christmas to hear the soft chiming of jingle bells? Make your own bells and hang them in a windy place.

You will need

- 3 paper cupcake cups (assorted colours)
- 3 small bells
- 3 pieces of yarn (red or green, 8, 10 and 12 inches each)
- 6 round gummed reinforcement *

- One toothpick

Get started

1. With the help of a toothpick, poke a hole in the centre of each cupcake cup.

2. Paste a gummed reinforcement over each hole on either side (inside and outside) of the baking cup.

3. Tie a bell to one end of each string.

4. Now run the other end of the string through the hole in each cup, so that the bell is inside the cup.

5. Tie the strings together at the top and hang the bells where the wind blows gently and hear them jingle.

 * Gummed reinforcements are self-sticking round paper stickers with a hole in the centre. They are easily available in any good stationery shop.

TOP CRAFTS

1 Table Decorations

2 Make Your Own Toys

3 Gifting Is Fun

Home Decorations

4 Fun With Weather

5 Home Decorations

Stain Glass Art

Make and hang a beautiful stain glass art piece in your room window.

You will need

- ⊃ Assorted kite paper
- ⊃ Craft paper
- ⊃ Paper craft knife
- ⊃ Craft glue
- ⊃ Thin cardboard or a thick sheet of handmade paper

Get started

1. Cut 30-40 squares (1 x 1 inch) of assorted kite paper.

2. Cut out a circle (7 inch radius) from the craft paper.

3. Trace out a pattern for the stain glass art, and cut it using a cutter knife.

4. Paste the kite paper squares to cover the circle. Overlap the squares a little (the blending of colours gives a nice effect).

5. Stick or hang it against a window, and admire your new room decoration.

Alternatively: You could even use coloured cellophane paper instead of kite paper.

Leafy Eagle

Would you like to hang a large, powerfully built bird of prey on the wall of your room?

You will need

- A light-coloured A4 size craft sheet
- Craft glue
- Dried leaves of different colours: brown, dark yellow, orange
- Sketch pens brown, dark yellow and orange

Get started

1. Take the A4 sheet and draw a rough sketch of the eagle on the paper (as shown).

2. Colour the head and the beak.

3. Paste dried leaves on the sketch. Start from the bottom and move upwards.

Paper Bandhanwar

Bandhanwar or traditional door hangings not only look beautiful but they are also supposed to ward off evil.

You will need

- Acrylic paint sheets
- Acrylic paints (for a glossy effect)
- Craft mirrors
- Craft glue
- Scissors
- Golden ribbon
- Beads

Get started

1. Cut out six *ambi* (mango) shapes and five semicircles (templates on pages 58, 59).

2. Draw patterns on these shapes.

3. Paint the *ambis* and semicircles with bright acrylic paints.

4. Decorate them with mirrors.

5. On a golden ribbon, alternately paste *ambis* and semicircles, with beads in between them.

Hang this on the entrance door, and it will catch everyone's eye!

3D Wall Decal Art

Perk up your room with these easy to make, beautiful wall decals.

You will need

- Coloured paper
- Craft glue
- Scissors
- Pencil
- Scale

Get started

1. Cut strips of 2 x 10 inches from coloured paper, for the flower petals. (One flower will have five petals.)

2. Paste the ends of the strips with craft glue and set them aside to dry.

3. Similarly, cut strips for the leaves.

4. Once the rings are ready, pinch each at opposite ends to make it look like the shape of an eye.

5. Arrange the flowers on the wall and start pasting with craft glue.

Below are a few variations:

Onion Print Snail

Can you believe that the ordinary onion can be used to create a cute onion-print snail?

You will need

- Medium size onion
- Brown, light pale brown poster paint
- Paint brush
- light green and dark green cartridge sheet (A4 size)

Get started

1. Cut the onion into half. The circles of the onions should be visible.

2. Keep it aside for about an hour for the onion to dry up a bit. The rings will show better now.

3. Keep a light green sheet horizontally on the table. Draw the body of a snail (as shown).

4. Colour the snail with brown poster paint.

5. Now take the onion, put some light brown paint on it and stamp it on top of the snail's body. Remove the onion and you will get a circular print like the shell of the snail.

6. Cut some grass from the dark green sheet and place it around the snail.

7. Draw the antennas with a dark black pencil.

Comb Effect Scenery

Set your pretty paper boats sailing, in this beautiful scenery.

You will need

- Light blue pastel paper (A3 sheet or coloured chart paper)
- Cobalt blue poster paint
- Paint brush
- Small travel size comb
- Origami paper for origami boats and fish

Get started

1. Spread the light blue paper on a flat surface, horizontally.

2. Draw a light line with a pencil, halfway up the sheet.

3. Now paint the lower half with cobalt blue poster paste (don't make the paint too thin so you can apply a thick coat).

4. While the paint is still wet, run a comb over it, in a wavy motion, left to right.

5. Now make origami fish and boats and paste them on the waves.

6. You could even add other features like the sun, birds, clouds etc.

Twig Tree

Make your own table top tree from real twigs and the remains of some gift wrappers.

You will need

- Twigs (pick these according to the size of the vase or flower pot in which you plan to place them)
- Waste gift papers/ wall papers (or any sturdy paper)
- Craft glue
- Scissors

Get started

1. Fold the paper in half and cut out 20-30 leaves from the gift papers. (If you are using double-sided thick paper, don't fold the paper. If the paper is thin or not printed on both sides, you may use double sided leaves for a better look.)

2. Paste the leaves on the twig. For thin paper, paste double-sided leaves.

3. Decorate the tree with lights and decorative hangings, during the festive season.

Alternatively: You can use old magazine paper for the leaves. Your leaves need not be green—go ahead and explore a multicolour tree.

Straw Art Lamp Shade

Decorate your old lamp shade with straws and give it a new look!

You will need

- Straws (white/transparent)
- Needle and thread (white / nylon thread)
- Yarn (white, or in a colour matching the straws)
- Light weight small beads (optional)

Get started

1. Cut 2-3 centimetre long straws.
2. String the cut straws horizontally. Make around 15-20 strands of straw (depending on the length and circumference of your lamp shade).
3. Make a knot or attach a bead at the end of each strand. Make sure the beads are small and lightweight.
4. Once you are done making the horizontal strings, take a yarn one and a half times the circumference of the lamp and join the straw strands.
5. Add more straw strands, if required, or evenly space out the strands and tie a knot.
6. Light the lamp and enjoy your new room décor!

Sandpaper Art

See this special seahorse come alive on paper. You can use this cool art idea for just about any art project.

You will need

- ⊃ Sandpaper
- ⊃ Multi coloured crayons
- ⊃ White sheet
- ⊃ Iron

Get started

1. Colour the sandpaper using various coloured crayons. You will need to press the crayons hard to be able to colour the sandpaper.

2. Trace the pattern of the sea horse. given here on white paper.

3. Invert the sandpaper (the coloured side) facing the sea horse on the white sheet of paper.

4. Take a hot iron and iron the sand paper. (Be careful and use adult help, if required).

5. Remove the sand paper.

6. Cut the outline of the seahorse.

7. Use this pattern on a card, gift tag, bookmark or just about anything.

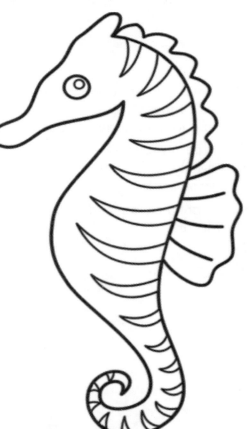

Rooster Book Holder

Stack up your favourite books by your bedside, with this funky book holder.

You will need

- Hanger
- Thermocol ball (available at a good stationery shop)
- 2 medium-sized googly eyes/ cloves
- Orange and red pipe cleaner
- Scissors
- Red craft paper
- Craft glue

Let's begin

1. Keep one hand on the centre of the hanger and the other on the hook and straighten and elongate the hanger as shown.

2. Lay the hanger on a flat surface, and leaving about four inches from the corner, bend both the ends of the wire up at right angles.

3. The hanger should be U shaped and the hook should face away from the centre of the U.

4. Push the thermocol ball on to the hook.

5. Make a slit on top of the thermocol ball to insert the rooster's comb.

6. Fashion a crown out of a red piece of paper and insert it into the top of the ball, for the rooster's comb.

7. Bend the orange pipe cleaner and push a small 'V' shape into the ball, for the beak.

8. Paste the googly eyes or insert cloves, for the eyes.

9. To use the book holder, place books upright in the rooster's back.

Iris Paper Flower

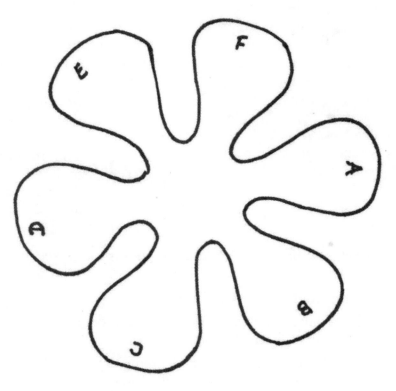

Caterpillar Arm Puppet

Leave space
to insert
your arm

Dancing Snake

Floating Ducks In A Pond

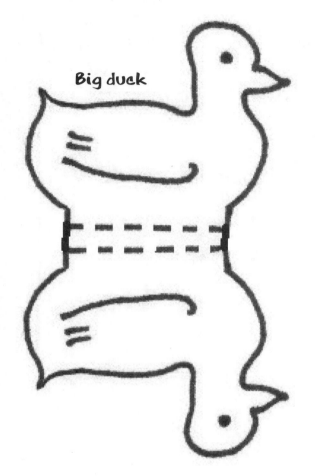

Big duck

Small duck

Flying Bat

Template

Tumbling Monkey

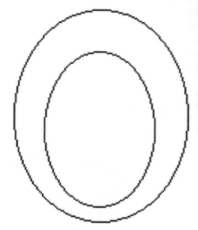

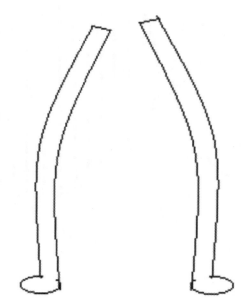

Parrot in a cage

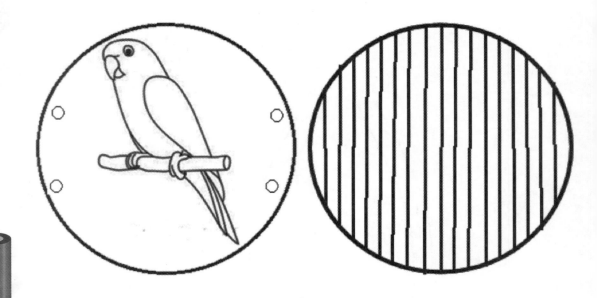

Flying Fish

Sun Catcher - Vegetable Stain Glass

Paper Helicopter

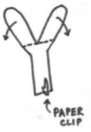

PAPER CLIP

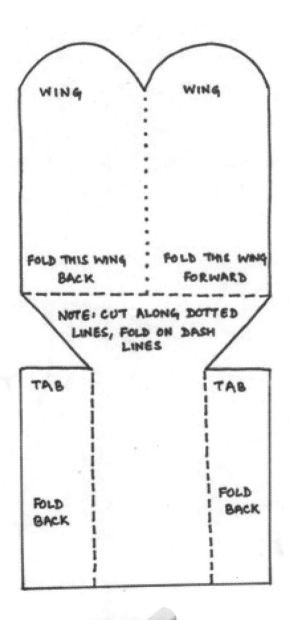

WING

WING

FOLD THIS WING BACK

FOLD THIS WING FORWARD

NOTE: CUT ALONG DOTTED LINES, FOLD ON DASH LINES

TAB

TAB

FOLD BACK

FOLD BACK

Bandhanwar

Bandhanwaar

Other craft activity books from Scholastic:

This and That
40 THINGS TO MAKE, DO AND TRY
Anitha Bennett

Forty fun-filled projects.

ISBN: 9788176554831
Pages: 104

More Paper Craft
Anitha Bennett

Make many unusual knick-knacks from paper.

ISBN: 9788184773910
Pages: 64

Paper Craft
Anitha Bennett

Make unusual gifts and knick-knacks from paper.

ISBN: 9788176555722
Pages: 64

Puppet Craft
Neetu Sharma

Learn to make different kinds of puppets.

ISBN: 9788184774733
Pages: 128

Toy Craft
HOW TO MAKE RACING CARS, GUITARS, PERISCOPES AND MORE
Neetu Sharma

Learn to make interesting toys with this exciting book of craft.

ISBN: 9788184776966
Pages: 120

Trash Crafts
EXCITING THINGS TO MAKE OUT OF JUNK
Benita Sen

Create many wonderful things from trash.

ISBN: 9788184770414
Pages: 96